JONES

Keeping Up

A S H   E R I C M O R E

All Rights Reserved. This is a work of fiction. No part of this publication may be reproduced, distributed, or transmitted in any form or by any means, except in the case of brief quotations embodied in critical reviews.

Written by: Ash Ericmore

Copyright © 2024 Ash Ericmore

Cover: Ash Ericmore

ISBN: 9798877316393

www.ashericmore.com
www.patreon.com/ashericmore

With Special Thanks To

Christina Pfeiffer, August Vaughn,
Crystal Cook, Jessica Shelly,
Donna Latham, Kimyona Dietter,
Christopher Ridge, Ugur Kutay,
Nat Whiston, Eddie Greenham,
Erica S, Emma Butler, Cat Goy

Want to see your name here? Check out

www.patreon.com/ashericmore

or

ko-fi.com/ashericmore/tiers

JONES

Mr. Jones

People will tell you that there are tricks to getting away with murder. There's only one I know of. I should know. The trick is simple. Act with some confidence. Pretend like you're supposed to be there. You're supposed to be doing that. You know? Like, they say, if you walk into a cinema complex carrying a ladder, no one will question you and you can just hunker down and watch a movie. Like that.

But stickier.

Take this woman in front of me. She's walking home from work, in the middle of the day, going for lunch. I'm following her. I'm not doing anything counter-intelligence wise—I wouldn't know how to—I'm not slipping in and out of doorways. I'm not popping different hats on. Christ. That would be funny, wouldn't it? No. I'm just walking a little way behind her down a fairly quiet road. I'm walking like I own the joint and I don't care. And everyone else— you see, they're the people that matter—they aren't paying me any attention because I look the part. I'm confidently walking down the street. On my way to a meeting. Going to buy fish and chips. Who cares what the destination is, it's the fact that I'm supposed to be going there. Furtive looks and careful steps ... that's what gets you noticed, my friend. And getting noticed, gets you remembered.

You remember back in the day when 'reconstructions' were all the rage, don't you? Crimewatch or something, that TV program with the presenter who got killed. Something like that, would put together … a reconstruction of a crime. Usually one like the one I'm about to do, and they would dress up someone like the victim and get them to retrace their steps and then some regular schmoe would be watching saying to themselves, *fuck me, I remember that*. And then some spark would fly and suddenly that schmoe is on the phone to Crimewatch telling them that they remember seeing that girl in a red dress walking along the line of shops with the bookies and there was this bloke. Following her. Looked furtive. He was tall. Looked like a cross between James Bond and Mr. Bean. Had a teddy, a bag of sweeties, and a Game Boy Advance. Bag with handcuffs and a dildo. And then *bam*.

Bang to rights.

You see? See how easy it is? You just need to walk like you own the place.

This woman in front of me. She's been going home for lunch every day from her job in the council offices at about the same time. She goes home. Spends a good thirty minutes there, and then heads back. I've been watching for a while. I've been sitting on the benches in the centre when she leaves, eating something from the chippie. Or a Maccies when the fancy takes. She leaves, I follow. No one see's me because I fit in.

I know she has an hour for lunch. No one ever goes with her. She never takes a call.

Some of it is supposition but, from that, I can assume she doesn't have any great friends at her job, and she doesn't need to check in with anyone. A little more of a stretch, but that also means that if she fails to get back to work on time, the boss might miss her, but very few others would. Now these days, the employee has all the power. The boss isn't going to call them straight away when they're ten minutes late back from lunch. Maybe thirty. Maybe an hour. It doesn't matter.

I'll be long gone before then.

In fact, when her lunch break finishes at one, I'll be gone. It isn't worth the risk. She won't be missed by *anyone* until then. When I've followed her back before, she stands outside until her lunchbreak is finished, before reentering the building, never giving the employer an extra second of her time.

So I have until the dot of one, before I have to be out.

Plenty of time, right?

I know. It's in the planning.

She's just crossed the road in front of me. About to turn right into her road.

I skirt over the road to the other side, so when she turns she doesn't see me. After she's turned, I walk over the mouth of the road, and then turn back, following her on the other side. She's a good distance ahead of me now, but that's okay. I'm prepared. I know where she is going.

She turns into her garden, up the path, and by the time I reach it, she's in. Gone. No one could possibly see me following her these last metres, because I wasn't following her. I was coming to the same location. There *is* a difference.

I stroll down the path, and I knock on the door.

When she answers, I smile. Looking all stern and angry never gets you anywhere, does it? I mean, put a smile on things and everything goes a little easier. Doesn't matter what. People treat you differently. I push my hand into my pocket and pull my I.D. "Good morning, my name is Dowdy, I'm from the council," I say.

"I work at the council," she says back.

I know. That's why it's perfect. "Yes." My smile widens. "I've seen you on the counter. Housing, isn't it?" A little bit of research goes a long way. I don't wait for an answer. "We've had a report from …" I pause, pretending that I'm thinking, "… someone about the boundaries changing at the rear of the property." Most people would say they are from the Gas Board or something. Way too obvious. "I was wondering if I could speak with you about it?"

She shakes her head. "I barely have a yard, I couldn't possibly have changed my boundaries. What does that even mean?"

I shake my head and sigh out with audible frustration. "I'm so sorry, it must be a different address." Shaking my head, I continue, "Do you mind if I just take a look? It'll just ensure no one else comes back and bothers you again. You know how these things can get out of hand."

She steps back and lets me pass.

If you're doing someone a favour then they tend to give you what you want. They let you in. Show you around. Give you coffee. *I've come to read the metre* tends to get an eye roll and questions.

I step by her and she closes the door behind me.

And I've got her.

I walk down the hallway towards the back of the property, quick looks at this and that. Nothing out of the ordinary, but I'm building a picture in my head of her. Her home life, her family. There are no pictures on the wall, but she's young. Probably doesn't go for that. Passing the living room, I see a TV, but little else. The small house is immaculately tidy. There is a fragrant smell. No dogs. No animals at all. At this point, I can still turn back if I have to.

Before, I've gotten to this point and found a fucking great dog there, circling the kitchen, and I've looked out the back and apologised profusely and left. Leaving her, no idea of how close she came to being gutted.

I reach the kitchen. "This way is it?" I ask. Politeness. It puts people off guard.

"Yes," she says. "Look." She was close behind me, now in front. I put the smile back on before she points out the window and looks back at me. "See? Nothing's changed."

I stand there next to her and look out the window. One final check to make sure I'm in the clear. I can smell her. As we stand there together. It's weirdly intoxicating. She's got a bitter perfume on. Flowers with something else. Leaning over the sink with me, her shirt is pulled tight over her breasts. Her long red hair hanging down. Almost in the sink, in the dishes from breakfast. I tut. "I can't apologise enough," I say.

"It's not your fault, is it?" she says. She steps back and away, allowing me to turn and leave.

I move hard and fast, backhanding her across the cheekbone. Feel the snap of her head as she rolls away from me. Back. To the floor. She lays there, stunned for a moment. The surprise is what gets them. There's no immediate realisation and leap to action. They're all the same. They slowly realise the awful truth. They realise they're in the house, alone with me. And they don't know who I am. *Am I a rapist?* they think. It's usually where the begging starts. There are sometimes threats. Sometimes promises. The big one is from the TV, where they all promise not to tell anyone if I leave right then. Which even on the TV is a pretty hollow promise. Tell someone? Like you're going to be around for that.

I stand over her, intimidating, I know. Waiting for the starting gambit.

"What do you want?" she says.

I never really know how to answer that one. Telling the truth seems so ... *violent*. "I want to know what you're willing to do to see me gone," I say. It's a stupid line, but it's what just came to mind. I have to admit, seeing them beg isn't so bad.

"What do you want?" she says, stupid girl. "You can have anything, just don't hurt me."

I nod. "Get on your knees."

She does. She thinks I'm going to want her to suck my cock. I've never understood rapists demanding that. Threats like, *no teeth or you'll get it*. Clearly screenwriters have never had their cocks bitten. *Ohhh ... nasty*. Anyway, in answer to your question, no, I will not be doing that.

This isn't about sex.

Sex is between me and my wife. It doesn't involve strangers ... often ... and I certainly am not putting my dingaling near this psycho's mouth. I can see the look in her eyes, she's already planning to bite my cock off. Look at her.

She gets dutifully to her knees in front of me and I step forward, closing the space between us. Then she goes to start working on my trousers. I bat her hands away. "No, no, no." I say. She looks a little confused. Then I lean forward, in one motion putting both of my gloved hands around her neck and squeezing.

She looks surprised at first. Like she wasn't expecting it. I blagged my way into your house and knocked you to the floor. What did you think was coming, flowers? Then fear comes. That's the one. That's the look I wait for. The jackpot. She looks scared that I'm going to kill her. Her hands on my wrists. At this angle, there is simply nothing she can do. She's on her knees. I have my weight over her. Without air she can't scream. Her eyes begin to bulge as she struggles to move, but I'm no slouch at this. I have her, and I won't let go, not until she stops moving. Her mouth, open as she gags for air. Her eyes widen just a little further, never leaving mine, until she finds the strength for one last attempt at finding escape ... but the cylinders aren't all firing by now. She's looking around for a way out. The only thing she could do would be to attack, but as the seconds drip by the chance of that gets thinner and thinner.

Until now. When there's nothing left in the tank and there's no life left. She lets go of my wrists, dropping her hands down, without air, there is no strength for that. Her body is trying to hold on, conserving the strength for survival. As I grip, just as hard now as when I first held her. One minute gone by, another to go.

I can feel her weight now in my arms. Her body is slumped. But the life is not gone. She's still holding on ... hoping. A subconscious act. Waiting for me to let go. At about one minute-thirty I see the life from her extinguish, and I wait just a few more seconds, before letting her go. At the drop of two minutes, I let her fall to the floor. Breathing hard. I feel great. I feel like I just won the lottery. I feel like I could just do it again.

I could.

But I have to hide my intent first.

I don't want the police ever finding out what makes me tick. Profiles lead to capture. So I like to mix things up. Keep them guessing. I'd love to be a fly on the wall when they find the bodies. I quickly look at the time. It's only twelve-twenty. Good. Plenty of time. I set my stopwatch—forty minutes—and start. I pull her to the table in the kitchen. It's a small thing. Wobbles when I drop her down. Cheap, but new. I've been thinking about replacing our kitchen table, and this just makes me want to die on my hill about getting an antique. My wife wants minimalist modern—whatever that means to a kitchen table—but I said I wanted a farmhouse table. Now, I'm sold. These modern ones are pants. I pull her clothing from her. Careful not to tear it, but quickly so I have time.

Once she is naked, I take a knife from the kitchen block. Cheap. Maybe the council need to look at raising the wage of their staff? She works—worked, sorry—from seven-forty five until four-thirty, with an hour for lunch and no breaks and can't—couldn't—afford a decent knife set? Damn. I look over the corpse. The clothes strewn around like I was trying to fuck her. What shall we go for this time? Sexual sadist? I look at the landing strip between her legs. Manoeuvre myself to there, and look at the knife. I push it, in between her legs, the blade facing upwards, twixt her lips. It's not sharp enough to cut through her at first, I get it in a good four inches before I reach anything that stops me. Then I saw it back and forth, pulling it upwards, watching as it cuts through the flesh. Without her heart beating her blood only drools out, sticky and damp, warm to the table top. Once I cut through, out the skin, splitting that strip of hair, I move myself around the body and cut up the corpse, a straight line towards the neck. I slit through the skin, to the organs, and then when I reach the sternum I bring the knife out and just cut through the skin. When I reach the neck I leave the knife, stuck into the flesh there, and pull her apart like a pair of curtains. The smell is horrid. I hate the smell of blood. It's like licking a spoon so much that you can taste the metal coming off.

Most unpleasant.

Reaching in I grab a handful of some intestine or another. I'm not a doctor, and I don't know exactly what it is. I pull it out, and tie a bow in it. Leaving it resting there on the body. See what they make of that, shall we? A corpse, fucked with a knife and then split in half and tied like a present.

Fuck. It's nearly ten to one. I leave the knife where it is and wash up in the sink. I know I'm leaving all sorts of DNA everywhere, but I haven't had so much as a parking ticket, I've never signed up for Ancestry or anything like that. My DNA is nowhere else apart from in my body.

Making sure I haven't left anything, I go to the front door. Check out the window. Then I leave.

One thing you have to be triple careful of these days is dash-cams. One car going by and you're on film. Bang to rights.

I check the time as I walk back towards the carpark in the centre. Twelve-fifty seven. Not bad if I do say so myself.

MRS. JONES

Fuck. Fucking hell. I can barely feel it. Is it in yet? Christ. I look down at Jeff. I think his name was Jeff anyway. He's laying on the bed. Grinning like he just won the lottery. He's thrusting his hips like a fucking baby, and clearly has no idea what he's doing. I shouldn't have changed the plan.

Normally, you see, I'll pick up a middle aged man. Someone about forty, towards fifty. Someone desperate enough to be eager to fuck, unhappy in the marital bed or something, but someone with the knowledge and skill to be able to at least put on a show for me. Then, I bring him to the hotel room and we fuck for a couple of hours and then I can be on my way.

But no, today I decided to grab a young man. He's got to be fifteen years younger than me, if a day, and he has no idea what he's doing. The hotel room was a waste of money. His, but still. And I'm just not feeling it. *Literally*.

I climb up him, from straddling him to getting myself nearer his mouth. "Eat me," I command, when he doesn't immediately start. He laps at me like a dog. Jesus Christ. He doesn't know where it is. Who's teaching these boys this? I should start teaching classes. On Only Fans maybe. But then who's going to get them to watch. Probably rather watch a couple of girls—who *do* know what they're doing—doing it to each other.

And that won't teach them anything. That much I

can guarantee.

I withdraw from the pointless tongue area. He's grinning again. He probably thinks he's some stallion. Pulling an older woman in the pub at lunchtime. Getting laid in a hotel room. I'm only thirty-five, thank you very much. I start to finger myself, try to get something started up at least, and reach around behind me to feel him. I touch his cock. He does have one at least, just doesn't seem to know where to put it. I give him a tug. He pulls this face like he's going to come. Shit. I hope he's not a virgin.

"Yes," he grunts out between breaths.

Fucking hell, he *is* ready to come. Fuck me. "Don't you dare," I snap. I slap him across the face. I want to position gold. Not fucking him. I finger myself faster, finding a rhythm when he starts to squirm because I haven't gotten him off yet and he thinks he should be getting some. Someone should teach this boy some manners. I guess that should be me.

He probably wants to come like they do in porn.

I find an orgasm down there in the dullness of this encounter and I make it bloom with no help from Jeff here. I lean over him and push down his shoulder, looking into his eyes as I come hard, shuddering over him. He wasn't good enough for me to squirt, but he doesn't care. He's just looking for *his*.

I pull myself off him and pull him up so we're sitting on the bed together. "You were amazing," I lie. "What do you want?"

He looks down me like a piece of meat, his grin returning after the disappointment of him not coming yet had smeared a slightly lost child look on his face. "Suck me ... no," he frowns. I might have broken him. "I want to come on your tits."

Wow. The choice of anything and he wants to knock one out over me. I've half a mind to tell him where to go and to leave. Then he could just do the same thing, but without me.

But I guess that would defeat the point.

I slip back and to my feet, getting from the bed and wave him forward, him following, knowing what to do now we're reconstructing a porn scene. He stands over me, and tugs on his cock. I push my titties together to catch it. Mouth open. Jesus. I wonder if the girls his own age let him do this, or if it's just because I asked?

He's slapping back and forth on his cock now, like he doesn't even seem to know how to get *himself* off. I cheer him on, phrases like, "Come for me baby," and "I want it all." I guess. I mean, I'm sort of thinking about the shopping list now.

Then he comes.

It dribbles from him. He's young. That shit should squirt from him. Maybe he just wasn't that into it? A girl can't help but feel a little hurt. It mostly slips down his hands and I end up sucking some of it from his glans, because I feel sorry for him. Then I stand and I push him back onto the bed. I let him lay there, huffing and puffing like a ... well ... a porn star ... while I pull a half bottle of brandy from my purse at the end of the bed. I pour a healthy triple into the glass that comes with the tea set and hand it to him. "Relax," I say. "I'm going to wash up."

I go to the shower and shut the door. I drop the lock, quietly. Stand and look myself in the mirror. I have virtually nothing to clean up. I shake my head at myself. And then I run the shower.

The water is warm as I step under. Careful not to wet my hair too much, I wash, thinking. Wondering what he would be like in twenty years. I wonder if he could have become a doctor. Or a mechanic. A shelf stacker. You don't know, do you? I mean some men take longer than others for their true colours to come out.

Not that it matters now.

I turn the shower off and step out, wrapping a towel around me. I look at the time on my phone. Fifteen minutes. I unlock the bathroom door and step out.

Jeff lays on the bed. His eyes staring up to the ceiling. His face gurned in terrible, terrible pain. The brandy spilled on the mattress. His hands clasped on this chest. The addition to the brandy is a little concoction of my own. It basically brings on extreme cardiac arrhythmia. It causes the person drinking it to have a heart attack. It has a pretty short half-life too, in alcohol. No more than a day. So by the time they do an autopsy, there is no evidence of me whatsoever.

I don't know why I want men to die after we've fucked. It's just something I can't help. An urge … a need. A warm glow rides up my body even now as I look at him. The corpse turning me on. I could just masturbate right now, watching him, but I won't. I'll just think about him while I'm fucking my husband later. Tonight.

I step around the room gathering my clothing and I take it all back to the bathroom to dress. Once back to an *organised* me, I return to the room. I leave the glass. I leave the bottle.

Then I leave the room. Downstairs, back in my business attire, I leave without looking back and no one notices me.

Have you ever noticed that? If you just walk about like you own the place, no one ever questions you? They never even remember you.

MR. JONES

Timing is important too. I turn the keys in the car and still the engine. Look up at the house. It's as *in place* as I am. A small suburban house in a side street. Neighbours think I'm quiet. You know. Typical serial killer. I slip out the car, and I straighten my shirt.

Close the car quietly, and go up the path to the door. It's a semi, so I do worry about the noise. I don't want my neighbours upset.

The Smiths.

Lovely couple. They have a little boy. He's a plumber and she's a marketer of some sort. I don't remember what exactly. She did tell me last Christmas when they were round for drinks. Something where she can work from home, but do as many hours as she wants. I don't know. Not really important, is it? A quick glance at the time as I open the front door. The warm air of the house drifts out and I slide in. Into the warm. It's welcoming, you know. I close up and head straight to my office. My office … listen to me. It's the second bedroom. A box room. I don't know how anyone was expected to use it as a bedroom, even for a kid. Pokey little thing. But no, *my office*. I hang my jacket over the rail at the bottom of the stairs where it was before I went out, slip my shoes off, slippers on. Up the stairs. Gerald passes me on the way. He looks at me, a questioning stare with his head to the side, before continuing off, doing his rounds, as the wife would say.

I sit, open my laptop, and look out the window

while it does its business. Self-employed, you see. I get to set my own hours, and nobody cares as long as I get the job done. I watch the street below, the cars trundling by every now and then. The road is quiet, usually. My mind slipping off to see it full of police cars, someone on a bullhorn, shouting at me to come out. That's how it's going to end, isn't it? They'll find something on me one day. Then I wonder how I'll take it. Will I give myself up? Will I go out in a blaze of glory, or will I down as many pills as I can lay my hands on and hope for the warm grip of death to take me before they kick the front door in. Which inevitably leads me to the question of life after death. Is there anything else?

I'm fucked if there is. But it's too late to worry about that. I suppose asking for forgiveness on my deathbed is probably out of the question.

My laptop dings at me and I'm taken from my thoughts. Look at the screen. It's a notification that I should be getting ready to end the work day. I love working for myself. Fancy a personal day? Fine. Done. I flick the notification away and look at the time. I should probably think about putting dinner on soon.

I open Youtube.

In a bit.

———

Never being a chef—I can barely make cereal—I've put a frozen meal in the oven. Stabbed the top and everything. I love the sound it makes. I fill a wine glass and place it on the table and await my wife's return. She works hard. It's all I can do to ensure she has a lovely meal and a glass of wine when she gets in.

Music plays on the stereo, drifting through the house, a warm embrace of home life. Something she hopefully looks forward too. I stroll to the front window in the living room and look out to the street again. I love people watching. The clouds are grey and I wonder if it's because its winter, or if it's just getting dark.

It'll be Christmas soon. I love Christmas, too.

Her car pulls up behind mine, and I slink away from the window. I don't want her to catch me watching. I don't want her to think I've been spying on her. I just go to the kitchen and busy myself until she gets in, in the house, coat off, as I listen, then she comes to the kitchen and kisses me without word. Her arms around my neck. We sink into each other for a long moment, before she slips from my arms and takes the glass of wine on the table. She takes a long glug, before returning it to the table and turning, leaning her arse on it, and smiling. She has a cheeky smile, and I hope that means she's had a good day. "Good day?" I ask.

Her smile widens a little. "Never bad. You know what the office is like. Busy-busy. I got a case today that is abysmal ..." she pauses, "... but I won't bother you with the hurdy-gurdy of the day. How about you?"

"Boring," I answer. I won't bother her with the details either. Heaven forbid. I smile quietly to myself, my secrets, mine.

"What?" she asks, seeing my coy little smile. "What have you been up to?"

"Christmas soon," I tease, turning to cover my grin. Lying is easy in November and December, isn't it? Everything that comes in the post is a secret, everywhere you go is a secret. And no one asks any questions. Being a home worker, though, it's all very easy for me. I crouch and look in the window of the cooker, like I'm Jamie fucking Oliver or something. It's a black plastic tray with something in it, covered in film … film that blackens and crinkles. I hear her sit and the glass going down again. "It won't be long." I get up and round the kitchen, placing my hands down on her shoulders and massaging them gently. Her head rolls and lets out a little groan of pleasure. I can smell something on her. Something I'm not used to. "New perfume?" I ask.

She shakes her head. "No, why?"

"I just wondered," I say. Doesn't smell right. I try to remember what she smelled like before she left this morning. It wasn't like this … I don't think. Shit. I can't …

"What's wrong?" she asks, my hands laying limp on her shirt as I think.

"Nothing," I say, trying to lighten my tone. I continue to touch her. Massage her. Maybe it was nothing.

It was probably nothing.

"Dinner smells nice," she says.

I grunt affirmation. It does, does it? Fine. I stop what I'm doing and round the table back to the cooker and take the plates from the cupboard. Put them in the warming tray at the bottom of the oven, and turn. I pour myself a glass of the wine for the first time. As she watches me. She has a look in her eyes. "I'll dish up in a second," I say.

Turning back to the cabinets and getting the rest of dinner on the go.

It wasn't great. I'm going to be the first to admit it. It was a ready meal and that about summed it up. But the film is good. After dinner we both loaded the dishwasher, before retiring to the living room and slumping on the sofa to watch the news headlines, and then some action film. It was her choice, and I am absolutely fine with that. I poured us both a spirit before I sat, for my wife a gin, and whiskey for myself.

The film is about halfway through, and we've both finished our drinks, I'm sitting in the corner of the sofa and she's laying against me. Propped up. The hero of the movie—a Jason Statham wannabe, I don't know his name—has just leaned on the bad guys and rescued the dame. They've gone back to his place because the villains won't know where he lives, and she's clearly going to make it up to him. For dragging him into this shit, or however they're going to phrase it. Weird, isn't it, that these action heroes are always the strong, silent, loner, type? Never see one that's married. Saves the girl, and when she says *let me make it up to you*, and starts pulling open his trousers, he says, *sorry luv, the missus is making shephard's pie tonight*. But I guess that would take the need for the obligatory sex scene. Not that I'm complaining. I get to see her strip off and flounce around the screen for a while and my wife can ogle the rippling Mr. Not-Statham. Speaking of …

She'd just dropped her top off, no bra. Amazing that, isn't it? Maybe I'm supposed to think she lost it in the toilets before they got to it. In some sort of anticipation … because bugger me if she wasn't wearing one when that warehouse exploded in the last scene. I'd have noticed if she was jiggling about all over the place.

Silly continuity. That's just for Shakespeare, isn't it?

My wife is stroking the front of my trousers as Not-Statham nails … oh fuck, whatever her name is. It doesn't really matter, does it. Pew-pew, then bang-bang, then more pew-pew. I could write films, you know. She squeezes her fingers around my cock, as it responds to her movement, as neither of us speak, nor do we stop watching the couple on screen fuck. I can feel myself getting more excited at her touch. She's always known how to turn me on. My arm is over her, and I slip my hand to her neck, caressing her flesh, feeling the goosebumps rise, before I turn her head from the screen and kiss her.

We embrace there on the sofa, teasing each other, tongues intertwined, before we go to the bedroom, the TV left playing to itself. It's okay though, it's on streaming and I'll be able to watch the rest of it tomorrow.

As we climb the stairs, hand in hand, she pushes against me, hurrying me to the top. To the bedroom, where she slowly strips me, pulling every article of clothing from me gently and slowly.

Then I strip her.

Just as carefully, not disturbing her skin with mine, the clothes coming away, until I can look at her body, beautiful. I lead her across the carpet to the bed, laying her down, and I crawl there next to her, my fingers caressing her body, in the warmth of the room. Minutes turning into an hour of me touching her. Bringing her to orgasm with my fingers, then my tongue, before finally, we make love. I do it all, she's tired after work and I've only exhausted her further.

I make sure she reaches orgasm one last time before I allow myself to the finish. And then we lay there, tenderly stroking each other until she falls asleep. Then I slide from the bed, naked, and aching … I tidy the clothes in silence. I shower quickly. Check the house, the windows and doors, and turn the lights off, going back to bed. As I slip into the sheets, she half-rolls onto me, grumbling, like she missed me in her semi-slumber. Then she's gone again.

Off into sleep.

I flick the light off, and stare at the ceiling in the blackness.

Every time I close my eyes I can see the police outside the window in the street. Surrounded. A man with a bullhorn. They're coming for me.

Sleep takes me eventually, but it is poor and not restful. I should see a doctor ... but tell them what?

M R J O N E S

The alarm goes off, and I bat it with my hand. Blinking my eyes open, I look at the time on the alarm clock, even though I know it's six. I hold my stare on the ceiling for a moment, and then pull myself from her arms. Standing, naked, I stretch. She grumbles, and turns over. I leave the room and go downstairs. Put the kettle on.

The garden, out the back, the sun just coming up, I watch the trees over the back moving. I can't feel the cold, but I *feel* the cold. I find myself staring into the garden until the kettle clicks off. The burning steam rising into the air. Pouring the coffee I go to take it back upstairs, when I see Gerald standing by his bowl. Staring at me. "Shit. Sorry little man. I'm half asleep." The mugs back on the side, I prepare the little dude some soft food. One pouch. He'll eat half now, and then by the time I come down at lunchtime the other half will be gone.

I pick up the mugs and take them up. Wake her up and we sit, quietly drinking coffee. It's a serene quiet, not in the least bit uncomfortable. Both of us having *staring time*.

After which the day begins.

I get ready, a shirt, suit trousers, I have no meetings today, and I don't plan on going out, and she dresses in her suit for work.

Then we head down, have breakfast. She likes to have something small and hot—I always joke that she can have me. She always laughs. A couple of rashers of bacon and some egg. No carbs. I make it, of course. Having my breakfast, more coffee. She leaves for work and I take my coffee into the living room and flick on the TV to watch the news before I start.

I'm on the news. Not me, per se, but my handiwork. I didn't expect it to be honest. I thought it would take them a couple of days, maybe. Clearly someone missed her. I wonder who found her. Her mother perhaps. Bit of a shock. A boyfriend? It didn't look like there was a male at the house often. A girlfriend? That gets my mind going, before I stop thinking and continue to watch. I stare at the screen, but my mind sees the bullhorn. The police say they have a suspect in custody. I laugh, just a little. They're flailing, taking anyone into the station. I do wonder who they got. That was number six. I know they've put them together, the TV has told me so. So they can't have arrested this one's boyfriend or girlfriend or mother or father … or *whatever*. They must have pulled some poor Johnny from the street and called him a likely lad and slung him in the cells. Probably shitting it.

The TV says that the girl was pregnant.

I drop my head to the side. Shit. If I'd known that I would have done something with it. Dragged out her uterus and framed it. I don't know anything about the reproductive cycle and woman's anatomy, so if that's wrong, sue me.

I can find out where you live. You remember that.

Anyway. Something like that. She was well liked,

apparently. Aren't they always though? You never see it on the news, do you? Mother of two hit and killed by drink driver. But it's okay, she was a bit of a cunt. God, that would be funny.

You know, if the news told the truth.

The financials come on and the murder is brushed under the carpet for now. My ears prick up. Shush. I need to pay attention.

Work is hard today. I keep staring at the screen, and then out the window. The thing is, I've been struggling not to up my game. Increase the timeframe.

To kill again.

I want to. I've always wanted to, but I've always pushed it down, deep into my gut. I have to be careful. I don't want people to know it's me. Hell no. Then they'll lock me up and I won't be able to do it anymore. But that's not the reason, really, is it? I mean, I don't want her to have to face the stigma of being the wife of a serial killer, whether they take me alive or not.

It's not a good look.

She might lose her job.

I flick from my spreadsheet to the news, open. BBC. Best in the world. I look at the story, updating regularly. According to the Beeb they don't have a suspect. I wonder if they let the schmoe go or if the other channel got it wrong. I want to kill again, and the news isn't helping.

I look out the window. The police cars. Bullhorn. But what if I killed again, today? Then left it. That would throw the police. Break my routine. They might think I'm escalating. Throw them into panic. Plus, it would quell my desire.

I could do it, just this once.

Sitting back, I look out the window. An old man is going by. He's got one of those walkers with wheels on, thumping and bumping against the uneven pavement. I've seen him before. I think he lives down the road.

I could do him. Go now, and follow him to the house. In. He must live alone, if he's out doing this by himself. It looks like a struggle, so he can't have live in assistance. He wouldn't fight back and I would be in and out in minutes. It's a bit close to home though. I shake my head. I do usually do women, though. It would be such a departure, what with the time and all, that the coppers might not think it was me. Put it down to a member of the family trying to get in on some copycat serial killing and getting the old man's house.

No, if I'm going to do it again today, I need to do a woman. Stay within most of my boundaries, at least.

MRS. JONES

I breathe quietly while Jonathan from upstairs lets out all of his frustration on me. He's venting, and whether he knows it or not, belittling me in front of my team. I can see him in my mind's eye, naked and writhing in pleasure, before I get my cocktail out and give him a glass. His cold fingers dropping the glass as his muscles relax without blood flow in the body.

"The figures are ..." he struggles for words. Then he blurts, "Fucked." He tosses the manila file to my desk and storms off. Point made.

I look at the file, and then to Tracy, the only member of the team brave enough to look at me. She smiles, weakly, passively, like she's sorry. I shake my head. "Don't you worry about it," I say, "you're figures are perfectly okay. He's just a jumped up little Hitler who wants to throw his weight around before he gets pulled up by the board to explain. I'll make sure they all know who is really at fault." Her smile broadens a little and she turns back to whatever she was doing. She's been in my team for a while now. Nice girl. She has a few problems at home that I know about, and I've been meaning to take care of them. Listen to me. Them. *Him.* Her boyfriend, Aaron, I met him at the Christmas do last year. He was an arrogant prick, and made eyes at me. In front of my husband, no less. Anyway, Tracy comes to work sometimes and I can see she has bruises. She tried to hide them, sure. But I saw them. You can't hide that sort of shit from me. Bruises on the arms where she's banged in on a cupboard. I can *see* the finger marks. A bruise on the face, covered with makeup. If you're coming into the office with completely different makeup, someone is going to notice, and I did.

Yesterday's dalliance will sate me for a while, but I can always break my rules. If it saves her from getting another beating. I don't want to keep doing young men though. Eventually it will raise suspicion if they keep dying of unknown heart problems. The older men, sure. I can rock that boat all night long. Someone in their fifties, or even older, having a heart attack shortly after sex. The whore, missing.

But I don't want to raise suspicion. Since the local killings have risen, I've flown under the radar. Imagine what it would do to my husband if he found out I was some freaky black widow. It would destroy him. He's so kind and gentle. Wouldn't hurt a fly. I realise that I'm staring into space and Tracy is watching me. I smile at her.

Go about my work.

I look up her personnel file though, just in case. Get her address. I know they live together, and someone like him ... he is hardly going to have a job, now is he? It's close. Close enough that I could do the deed in my lunch break and not even have to tell anyone I was at a meeting. Just slip out and fuck him and kill him. I suppose I could just kill him without the fucking, but that's part of the ... part of the *what*? I'm not even sure myself. It's just something I have to do. I'm drawn to it. The whole thing. Every few months, I have to do it, or I'll go mad, I just know it.

I shake my head. Note down the address, and move on. I don't need to kill right now. I don't want to. I don't know who I'm trying to convince. Myself, perhaps. I think about Jonathan again. I could kill him. So why couldn't I kill Aaron?

I don't want to. That's the end of it.

———

As I sit on the wall surrounding a tree in the town centre, the McDonald's Wrap of the Day in my hand, I stare. I watch the people. I watch the men. I don't know what drives me to it.

There is a group of police people, what are they called? The provisional lot. They're handing out leaflets and talking to the public about the serial killer. I don't care. I don't know anything about it, and it's not about me, and my *extra-curricular*. I stuff some more of the wrap in my mouth. It's getting cold, but you have to eat the fries first, don't you? Christ, if he caught me eating this, there would be hell to pay. I'm supposed to have a salad for lunch. I smile, chewing, watching a man about ten years older than me walking by. He has a cane, but I think it's for style purposes, not because he needs it.

I imagine myself riding him.

Feel that spark between my legs.

I don't know. Maybe I *could* do Aaron. Make everything better for her, and me at the same time. I tell myself I don't want to. Again. If I keep telling myself that, maybe I'll believe it.

MR. JONES

Her. That's the one. I've gone one town along to look, and I'm sitting in the car in a pay and display car park. There's a woman walking across the road. She's coming towards the car park, that's for sure. She's got a bag from Boots, the chemist. I watch her as she walks over to a small car. I don't know what it is, I'm not one for cars. She opens the boot and dumps the bag in without concern, then she gets in and pulls out.

I follow her. Following someone in a car is just like following them on foot. It's a piece of cake. You just drive behind them. Unlike the films they're not a savant cop who instinctively knows that there is someone tailing them. Think about it. The last time you were in a car—was someone following you? You don't know. You probably only looked in the mirror once. If that. You're a bad driver.

Whatever.

She turns into the High Street, and follows the road through to the other end, then out, towards the nice houses down at the bay. All I've got to do is be sure that the house is empty apart from her before I knock and I'm in the clear. One quick one. Get rid of the nagging need, the want that's scratching at me. And throw the police a bone they won't be expecting and put them further off the trail. Confound their profilers. Assuming they have them. I mean, I guess they have them. I know they have them in America. I don't know if the bum-fuck hippy coppers down here have that shit for sure. They might still have a pin board and Charlie Day pointing at it. You've seen the meme, right? She stops at the traffic lights and I pull in behind her. I think she's looking in the mirror at me for a second, then I realise she's checking her makeup. I tap the steering wheel out of anxiety, and whistle tunelessly in the silence until the lights change.

Then we're away.

Over the railway bridge, and down, passing the small row of village shops. I told you it was nice down here. Village-y feel. The bay is nice, the paths are wide. It's expensive down here. I've always wanted to live in this area, as it happens. She turns off the main drag into a side road and then into the short driveway of one of the first houses.

I pass the driveway and go to the end of the road, turn around and come back before she's even out of the car. I pull up on the other side of the road and get my phone out. Pretend to be doing something with that. No one sees me because it's all normal. Natural. Everyone has their face in a phone these days. She gets from the car, goes to the front door. She's forgotten the bag in the boot. She reaches the door, flounces, then turns back, gets the bag from the boot and then back to the house and in. I check my mirrors. Check around. Most of the people down here will be at work. Maybe the odd housewife fucking the pool boy. Then I turn my attention, subtle as it is, to the house.

Double fronted, and a gated drive. The gates stay open. They're not electric or anything. They probably never shut them. The car is parked at such an angle that another car could park next to it, indicating that there is someone else, out. Perfect. I open the car door, and taking my phone amble across the road, over the front of the house and around the corner. Check it from all sides.

I don't see anything out of the ordinary, but this isn't my usual M.O. Apart from anything, I'm usually much more careful than this. Either way, I'm pretty sure she's alone now.

I go back around to the front of the house. I'll wing it once I'm inside.

Go to the door and knock. Gently. I keep my phone in my hand and wait. She opens the door a moment later. I try to be engaged more with the phone than her, like my life depends on it, but it's hard. She's stunning up close. Like Samara Weaving, but hotter. I try to stay in character. Keep the pretence up. If I come across as a creeper on the doorstep, then I'll never get over the threshold. She doesn't speak. One of those. She just raises her eyebrows at me. Posh totty. Or arrogant, one of the two.

"I'm sorry to bother you," I say, "but my phone's all jacked up, and I can't get the app open." I shake my head. "The company thinks stuffing everything on a phone will increase productivity, but you let me tell you, it doesn't." I look at her expectant, all part of the act, then I continue. "Oh, I'm sorry. My names Cole." I pull my I.D. and hold it out. "From the Gas Board. You got a letter last week."

She looks confused, unsurprisingly, and looks

behind her, like someone might be standing there holding a letter. "My husband usually deals with that," she says.

"Oh, I'm sorry. Bad time? I just need to inspect the rear of the property for gas lines." I smile and indicate with my phone, pointing it behind her. "May I?"

Confounded she agrees and steps aside. Rookie mistake.

I pass and go through the house. "Nice place you have here," I ramble on, "shame to get it sticky."

"What?" she says, close behind.

"What?" I reply turning to her. I raise my hand and smack the woman as hard as I can on the cheek. I feel the bone splinter under my strike, and she looks stunned as her head snaps to the side and she tumbles to the floor. "Sticky," I say. She doesn't respond. I'm not surprised with how hard I hit her. Her face, reddened and starting to bulge already. I'm not a rapist. Never have, not once, even though the opportunity has arisen, time and again. But as I look down on her, I can see the appeal. Hitting her had brought my need to the fore. I want to hurt her, but I've never seen anyone so attractive. Laying on the floor. My gaze down on her. Her nose weeping blood. My eyes dance down her body as I watch. Lost a little in the moment. I look at the slate floor framing her. It's almost a renaissance painting, or would be if it wasn't for that bright red bowl.

I look at the bright red bowl disturbing my art, and wonder for a second why there is a bowl of water on the floor in the corner of the kitchen. It has the name Ralph written on it. I look up. Across the kitchen and circle slowly. The back door is a jar. In the garden looking across at me is a dog the size of a horse. As I smile at it, it starts to run at the back door. I have a split second to make the decision—try to beat it to the back door and close it, or flee. My flight response kicks in and I run for the front door. Fuck. She's not dead. She's seen my face. What have I done? I hit the front door bouncing my shoulder off it as I fumble for the handle. I can hear the footsteps—pawsteps?—of the animal coming. The fucking thing doesn't bark.

Not once.

It's going to tear me to pieces in silence and all this woman is going to find when she wakes up is bits of the gas man all up the walls. I might be in full panic. I don't know yet, no time to think. Fuck the handles or locks or whatever. I turn and boot the dog. It doesn't whimper. Takes it in its stride, like a champ. Sort of bounces back and thinks before readying to charge forward. I run from the immensely complicated front door and to the stairs. Up. Two at a time with fucking silent Cujo after me. To the top. In the first room. Thing biting at my feet. I slam the door and lean against it.

Fuck. What the fuck? Balls. See … do you see what I mean about planning? If you don't plan, then shit like this happens. I wait, not moving from the door, and look around the room. Catalogue my thoughts. She won't be out for long, I didn't hit her that hard. I'm on the first floor, with a healthy drop to the garden below, if I can work out how to open the window. I haven't done anything serial killer-y, so the cops might not put two and two together. There's a dog blocking my way. I can hear it scratching at the door to the ... I take in the room. *Master bedroom.* There's another open door on the other side of the room. A bathroom beyond. I glance at the photo on the nightstand. It's her downstairs. Then the picture above the bed, her again. Christ. I tenderly relieve the door of my shoulder, remembering that dogs can't open doors and I go to the window. Drop to the garden below? It's possible. I could drop down, and get to the front of the house and be away without Cujo knowing. Or I could shut the back door and lock it in the house. Find another way out of the garden. I go to the bathroom door and look in. Lucky I'm quiet. It's a Jack and Jill and the other door is also open. I slip in and to the other door. Looking out. The hall beyond and down there, Cujo, his tongue hanging out like he wants to play, drool slipping in globs from his maw. He's got a massive schlong, trailing across the carpet. He's sitting there at the door. Staring at it. Waiting to tear me limb from limb.

Or hump me. I don't know which would be worse.

The door across the hall is open. I don't suppose it has a fire escape though. So I close the door to the bathroom, waiting until it's nearly closed, and then I slam it. The dog charges up the hallway and scrabbles at this door now.

That should hold its interest. I hurry to the bedroom and look at the picture on the wall again.

She's naked. But it's arty. Yes. I definitely would. But I can't. I open the window and look down. There's the patio below. Great. Not even a soft landing. I climb through, carefully. I'm not built for this. I don't have the upper body strength of a baby. I get ready. Then boost myself off, away from the building and land on the patio below. I stand. Look around. I'm sure that I could be seen from the main road, but who is going to believe their eyes ... a man in a suit jumping from a bedroom window. Probably think I was fucking the missus when the husband came home.

I suddenly meet the eyes of her, now standing in the kitchen, holding her face. When she sees me, the two of us look into each other's eyes for a moment, like star-crossed lovers. Then she screams.

I burst into the house, limping from the badly disbursed body weight on my all-too spindly ankles and rush her. She doesn't move. She doesn't run. She Penelope Pitstop's. She cries and wails and waits for someone to fucking help. I barge passed her and slam the kitchen door, hearing the dog bounding down the stairs. I'm pissed off now. I just want this over, and I doubt that the kill will be anywhere near as cathartic as it was supposed to be.

I stand there staring her down, heaving air into my lungs, Cujo, scrabbling outside the door. I'm daring her to move. I limp to her, and she cowers. If she'd run she probably could have out-distanced me without a problem, but fear held her in place. And now I'm out for blood. She's not going to enjoy this. I wanted to fuck with the police profile of me.

Well get a load of this Plod …

I take her wrists in my hands and pull her close. Breathing on her. She's crying. Won't meet my eyes. I say, "I want you to strip naked so I can fuck you." She's got snot and blood oozing together on her face. But she nods. I let her go and step back, opening the draw behind me and grabbing the first thing I see that I can threaten her with. It's a roasting fork. Never used one before. She pulls her clothes off slowly. Trying to drag the process out, and maybe hoping I get bored and leave. Fat fucking chance, lady. You've seen my face.

She gets to her underwear and stops. Trying to cover her body with her hands. "Please," she's whimpering, "just go and I'll not call the police."

"Like fuck you won't." I wave the fork at her. "Naked," I said. Again. I hate repeating myself.

She nods. Pulls the rest of it off.

I nod, appreciating it. She has bruises on her ribs. I point with my fork again. "What's that?"

"Nothing," she says, too quickly. Covers them with a hand.

"Your old man beat on you?" I ask.

She looks at me and nods. "When I'm bad."

I shake my head. Some men are fucking pigs. This house is worth a fortune and this bird is a submissive goddess and this douche-canoe finds reason to lay into her. What a cunt. "Get on your knees," I tell her. She does. Lets her hands drop from her body. Thinks she knows what's coming next.

I stride over to her. "You're old man, cock is he?" I ask.

She lets out a little laugh. We're on the same team now. "Yes. I don't want to be with him. Would you help me with him?"

Hold on. Is this broad offering me a blow job in exchange for not killing her, but killing her husband? I consider it for the shortest of split-seconds. "No," I say. "It's not my problem." Then I bring the fork up and stab it down into her forehead. I let it go and stand back. She looks surprised. I probably look surprised. Even I didn't know I was going to do that. Now she's kneeling on the floor naked with a fork stuck in her head. She looks a little like a sexy unicorn cosplay.

I laugh. I can't help it. Blood starts to drool down her head, and I don't think she notices until she can taste it dribbling over her lips.

I then step back to her, take the fork and place my boot on her breasts. Pull the fork while kicking her back all *this is Sparta* like. She drops back to the floor, squirming in the blood slowly pooling under her. Painting herself a crimson red. I slouch down and stick the fork in her again. She's squirming so I don't bother aiming. It jams into her shoulder. I pull it, she screams. I stick it again. We dance that dance four or five times before I pierce something important and her noise become a moaning grumble, and she starts bleeding really hard. She still moves, a moving corpse, dashed in red. I stab again, and again until she stops moving. She's a flesh tea-bag by that point. More red on the outside than in. I watch her.

Breathing slowly. My shoes are caked in her goo. The dog stops scratching like it can sense it is too late.

Then I walk to the sink, and wash my shoes off.

Put them back on, and check her again. She's gone. I mean gone, dead. Bled out.

I leave through the back door, into the garden. Still limping badly, and tired. Dirty.

I let myself through the side gate, only bolted from the side, and then head back to the car. I get in, check my phone for messages, and then I head off, home.

MRS. JONES

I leave the office at lunchtime and head to my car. I jump in, and send a text to my husband, just to check in and see if he's having a good day. He must get lonely rattling about in that house all day by himself with only the cat for company.

I should surprise him one day and go home at lunchtime and fuck him senseless. Leave him in bed with a whiskey and a sore cock.

Starting the engine, I take the car out and head towards the address I'd written down for Tracy. I'm not going to do anything. I just want to look. To see if I *can* do something if I want to.

The traffic is bad, and I'm probably not going to get back to my desk in time. So I'll make something up. Some reason why I've been longer than an hour. A work reason. Something to do with that wanker, Jonathan, probably. I turn into the street and pull up down the road from the house. I check the address with the one I've noted down, about five doors down, and I stuff the paper into my pocket. I can see the front gate, and watch, check out the area. I don't usually do this … like *this*. It's usually more opportune. More of the moment. I don't plan. I'm just careful.

I see the gate of the house next door open and an old man come out. He walks away towards the other end of the road. Taking in the houses, I see they're all small, and quaint looking. They all have little gardens at the front and roses. It's nice. Not what I expected

Aaron to be content with. But from what I'd heard he only treated Tracy like a free ride anyway. I pull the car down the road a little, closer to the house. I can't see shit without getting closer, and I don't want to be caught. And I'm hungry. I should have picked up lunch on the way. Did a proper stake-out. I laugh to myself and start the engine again. I drive slowly along the road and over the front of the house. I watch through the window as I drive by, seeing him there in the front garden, just shutting the house up. I quickly look back to the road and carry on.

Definitely the right house then, so should I decide to come back, then I know where to come.

I just don't know if I want to.

I head along to the strip of shops down the road and go and buy a sandwich. Then head back to the office.

When I get back I tell Tracy that I've been in with Jonathon that whole time and I take my time, eating my sandwich and looking at gun ranges on the internet. I've always been fascinated by guns, but they're so hard to get a hold of in the UK. Maybe I should go to America. I could go to a gun range and see what's what. Maybe get one off the dark web. I smile through my chewing. I don't even think the dark web is a thing. I'll bet if I was to go there it would just be full of porn.

I should ask my husband when I get home. He's smart.

He'll know.

The afternoon was long and boring. When I get bored, my mind wanders and I found myself thinking more about Aaron than I should have. Seeing him naked on the bed, surprised and satisfied, and covered in cum, his heart no longer beating. His eyes … glazed and staring at the ceiling. My orgasm subsided, as I shower.

I breathe out, and shake the thought from me. It's raining, and my mind really should be on the road as it starts to get dark. Have you ever noticed how people drive like arsehats at this time of the night? Between schools chucking out and six? They all seem to think that if they can't get there in minutes, then they'd rather be dead.

I know I sound like my mum when I talk like that, but it's true. I laugh, shake my head and flick the Drive Time programme on. It's that blond woman talking. The one with the famous dad. She's saying that it's going to rain and the traffic is shit. Well, I couldn't have seen that coming.

It takes me longer than usual to get home and when I do, dinner smells ready, and there is wine waiting. I toss off my jacket, discarding to the stairs and go to the kitchen, my wonderful husband, a glass of wine. "Something smells good," I say, looking expectant.

He smiles back. "Liver and bacon," he says.

I like liver and bacon. We don't have it often

enough. I slip into a seat and take the wine. Sipping. It's cold, crisp. White even though it doesn't pair with liver, but is my preference. I notice him limping. "What have you done? Hurt yourself?"

He nods, but looks dismissive. Then carries on with the mash. "Did you fall over the cat?" I ask.

He shakes his head, "No, nothing like that. I just stumbled on the stairs."

He's lying. I don't know why, but I know that he is. I look around the floor for Gerald. He prances by with a catnip mouse in his mouth. Nothing wrong with him. Then I look back at my husband. He's doing the mash but watching me as well. He can see me being distrustful. But he's lying. I know it.

"How was work?" he asks.

"Boring as always," I reply. I want to know what the truth is, but I don't want to ask. If he's not telling me the truth, he must have good reason. Then he dishes dinner.

Dinner is nice, and the conversation doesn't go back to his ankle.

Then we retire to the lounge. I flick the news on, there's been another murder. "It's like the Channel Islands around here," I say.

"What?" he sips his drink getting into the corner of the sofa.

"You know, Bergerac."

"Who?" He's listening to me, but watching the news.

"The detective. From Midsommer."

"That community in the Netherlands?"

I shake my head and settle in. Then man on the TV is saying, " … jumped from the first floor bedroom window … about six foot in a dark suit."

"Could be anyone," my husband adds. "They'll never catch him."

"No," I agree. "Not a chance." All the better really. It's certainly keeping my going ons under the radar.

I snuggle down into the cleft of his shoulder and torso and keep the drink close to my lips, deciding to work out what is wrong with him later.

After the film we settled on finished—some Brad Pitt vehicle—we head to bed upstairs. He picks up my jacket from where I'd dumped it on the stairs and lays it carefully on the bed. We cross each other on the landing as I come from the bathroom and he goes in. Kissing, deeply and passionately as we do. Then I go to the bedroom and pick up my jacket. Tired, and a little disoriented from the alcohol, I pick it up from the bottom, and everything from the pockets tumbles out.

I pick up the loose change from the inside pocket—no idea how that had gotten in there—and push it back in, righting the jacket. I hang it on the front of the wardrobe to wear tomorrow, before picking up the papers from the other pockets and tossing them in the waste bin in the bedroom.

When he comes back to the bedroom, I'm sitting naked in bed, the sheets up tight around me, a book that I'm not reading in my hands as I stare off into space. Half thinking about what's wrong with him, his ankle, and the other half of me worrying about Tracy and the problems she has.

He climbs into bed and we cuddle naked. I can feel his hardness but he doesn't try to fuck me. We just hold. It's a warm feeling to be loved like this. The embrace is comforting, although I can't get the niggling feeling from my head that he's keeping something from me.

But I do sleep, after a while.

———

The alarm clock brings morning breath with it and I can't help but stagger to the bathroom, leaving my husband in the bed, warm and wrapped, burrito style. I stare myself down in the mirror before deciding to get on with it … the fleeting thought of calling in sick, brushed aside as I don't want to lose the pay. I ready myself for work, getting to the kitchen before he rises, leaving me to feed Gerald.

When he appears at the kitchen door I ask him if he's all right. I don't say it, but it's most unusual for him to be this slovenly in the mornings.

He grunts as he sits, lifting the coffee from the table. "Just aches," he says.

"Getting old," I reply, laughing it off. He doesn't

share the sentiment, clearly, as a grumble is all I receive in reply. "What you got on today?"

He shakes his head like he does know, or perhaps doesn't care. "The usual. You in the office all day?"

"Of course." I nod. Why would he think otherwise? I don't know. He's in a funny mood. I'll leave him to it. I pull my jacket on and kiss him as I leave. The passion from the night before isn't present, and I look at him more seriously as I pull away. "Are you sure you're okay?" I ask.

He nods, then turns his attention to his phone.

Like I'm chopped liver. I'll probe him later. Find out what the problem is. Maybe he's coming down with something, maybe he's having a problem at work that he doesn't want to tell me about. I don't know. I go to the car and get in, us barely speaking after that.

Turn the music up and listen to some Ozzy Osbourne on my way through traffic. *Crazy Train*, baby. I sing along, watched by the people in the next car at the traffic lights.

Fuck 'em.

I'm first into the office when I get there, and I sit at my desk, coffee in hand. Staring into space. There's nothing for me to do before I technically clock in. So I don't work. Why should I? I think about my husband instead. I want to help him with the problem, but I can't until he tells me what it is.

Then the boys come in. They greet me and sit at their desks, their jovial behaviour as they came in through the door diminishes as they sit, and they log on, starting work. It's not time to start work. Maybe they do because I'm sitting here? They don't have to, it's not time. Then one of the girls comes in, sits, and just as the clock ticks to the hour, in comes Tracy. I watch her in silence. I don't say anything about her bloodshot eyes. She's been crying and I know who is to blame.

But I bite my tongue. If she wanted to tell me she would. But she hasn't. I should keep my nose out of it, but I don't want to.

At about ten, I get up with some paperwork and take it to her desk, lean over her as we discuss it quietly. My vantage, allowing me to look over her. I can see purple and green from under the hem of her shirt. She's tried to hide it, but close up, they're fresh. He beat her before she came in this morning.

That's it. *Enough.*

I thank her and make my excuses. A meeting with Gerald at head office. Then I leave. I'm seething. So much so that I used my cat as an excuse. I go to the car, and drive to the house. I sit there and prepare the bottle of whiskey I picked up from the office licence on the way over.

Spike it with the powder I keep under the passenger seat.

Then I go to the gate, and take one last look at the house, before going and knocking. Aaron answers the door a couple of minutes later. A balled fist rubbing his eyes. He's just gotten out of bed, clearly, his robe hung loose at the belt, open, I can see his chest. He's not muscular, but sculpted, I suppose. Enough to impress teenage girls and beat on the missus.

He's got his hand held out to take something. He's not even looking at me. I stand there, waiting to be acknowledged.

"What?" he says, finally looking at me. There's no recognition, and he still thinks me a delivery man. Woman. What. Fucking. Ever. Just being in his presence angers me.

I smile through it. "Aaron?" I say. I flutter my eyelids like a teenager with a crush.

He blinks like a hungover buffoon. "Yes." His hand drops away, realising I'm not a postie.

"Remember me?" I ask, waiting a second or too, as he squints at me. "I'm Tracy's boss. We met at last year's Christmas do."

"She's not here." He waits a second like the words are still sinking in. "Shouldn't she be at work?"

"She is," I continue, apparently having to handfeed him. "I'm here to see you."

That seems to get his attention and he looks first like a startled monkey, and then like a cat that got the cream. It seems to awaken some un-before-seen persona. He leans up against the doorframe like we're at a disco, smiling … he winks. "And what can I do for you, love?"

Jesus Christ. I don't let my smile waver, even though I want to vomit in his face. That's the thing, isn't it? I usually pick and choose. I usually enjoy this part, almost as much as the next, but on this occasion,

I don't. But I have to go through with it, regardless. "I saw the way you looked at me last year. And I haven't been able to stop thinking about you." It doesn't make a lot of sense, but I doubt this Neanderthal will care. I'm putting my arse on a plate and letting him have it for lunch. Well, brunch, I suppose. It's a bit early.

"Yeah?" he says.

God. Anyone else would have at least invited me in. He must be cold. "I want you. Do you still want me?"

He looks me down like he's checking.

Fucking cheek.

Then he steps aside and allows me into the house. I step by him and let the tips of my fingers run over his chest. He closes the door and follows me, stopping at the bottom of the stairs. "Up?" I ask. He nods, apparently lost for words. I know it's a cliché, but this really, actually *never* happens in real life. He will have seen this play out in porn, yes, and once you reach about thirty, you realise that porn scenarios are just that. They don't happen-happen. Except this one is for him. For now. I climb the stairs and head to the bedroom. The house is small and I can find my way without guidance. There I aid him to sit on the bed, and step away from him. Slowly undressing. Not like stripping. No. In this situation, I'm the older woman. Needing his young cock. He doesn't care. Just sits there and watches. Silence.

I can smell Tracy's perfume in the room. A cologne, too. His. It's cheap and overpowering. The wardrobe is open, Tracy's clothing hung. I recognise the suit she wore last week. I take my skirt down, my body only covered by bra and panties. He readjusts his junk. Turned on. Good. I step to him and pull his robe open. He's naked beneath, semi hard. His hands on my body already, roaming over me, and tugging roughly at my panties. He has no class and no style and he wants the goodies. He's not a considerate lover like my husband, out only for himself. I'm not surprised. I stroke his cock hard, and let him pull my panties down.

Then I push him back onto the bed and we fuck. It's raw, hurts a little. His cock is not big, but he jabs it at me like I'm a blow up doll. I fake everything. Unconcerned by this part now. I just want it over.

And like that, it is.

He lasted maybe a minute or two. I screamed the house down. He seemed to like that. I imagine that Tracy lays back and thinks of England.

I slide from him. Feel his seed weeping weakly from me. I get the whiskey and hand him the bottle. Then I go to the shower. He's a pig and he'll drink it. From the bottle, I expect.

Then I wash him from me. The act done. I clean up, dry down and look myself in the mirror again, the second time today. I look lighter now, somehow. I've done something good, in the worst way possible.

I return to the bedroom and he's laying on the floor. I pick up the empty whisky bottle. He'd already drained it. I put it in my bag and drag him across the floor to the bed. I manage to half-pull and half-roll him onto the mattress. I wash his flaccid cock of after-spurt and vaginal trace. Then I cover him with the sheet. He looks like he's sleeping. That's the best way for Tracy to find him. A heart arrhythmia or something. Still laying in bed. She'll call the ambulance and it'll be *just one of those things*. And she'll be free. I dress and get all signs of me cleared away to my bag. The bottle. Cap. Then I go downstairs and check the house, make sure it's all locked up and I leave.

Back to work.

Like I was never there.

MR. JONES

I sit in the car my head leaning back against the headrest. I keep my eyes closed for some periods, waiting. Listening.

I was late getting up this morning.

That jump from the window did me in good and proper and I felt terrible letting my wife get up like that. I got from the bed and I pulled my dressing gown on. I picked up the waste bin from the bedroom, took it to the bathroom and I tipped it into the bin in there.

There was a paper, half crumpled with an address on it.

I wasn't spying on my wife. I promise you I wasn't. I thought it might be important, so I took it, and I looked at it. It was a local address. I don't know why, but something spoke to me. She'd been acting oddly last night. Like she was suspicious or something. I just stared at it for a minute, and then thrust it into my pocket and went down stairs.

She was acting like nothing had happened. Maybe it hadn't? Maybe I was paranoid. Maybe all those police, sitting outside my office window ... a dream about the bullhorn ... maybe it was all getting to me.

I drank my coffee and when she'd gone to work I came here. I sat in the car, and I waited. I just wanted to know whose house it was.

Then *she* arrived. I ducked down in my seat like some sort of undercover P.I., and I watched her go to the house and flirt with the man inside. I recognised him, and it took me a moment, but I realised it was that cunt from the Christmas party. What's-her-name's boyfriend. The one who'd made all those eyes at her.

She went in. Twenty minutes later and she's come out. She's fucked him. I just know it. I wait for her to get into her car and leave. I sit there in the car for a few minutes. My heart stabs with each beat. How could she do this to me? How could she be having an affair ... with *him*? He is a dickwad. A wankhank. A fucking .... Enraged I punch the steering wheel over and over, before getting from the car. Standing, I straighten, and I breathe in. I go over to the house and down the sideway to the back garden. It's like a character cottage. I check through the windows. Don't see him. Then I take a garden fork and jam it into the wooden window frame, forcing the window open. I listen, to see if he's coming, and when the coast is clear, I climb through, huffing and heaving. My ankle sore from the day before—ha, that rhymed—and my muscles ache. Into the kitchen. I can't believe that he hasn't heard me.

I grab a kitchen knife and start to search the house.

I'm going to gut him. That's what I'm going to do. After looking around the downstairs and not finding him, I slowly climb the stairs, imagining my wife doing the same only half an hour before hand. I get to the top and look around the doors—bedroom door half-open, nothing in the bathroom. I look between the crack and the door of the bedroom at the hinges and see his feet. Under the covers. That's proof. There, for all to see. I wait for a moment and he doesn't move, so I take the guess that's he's asleep. Probably is. The sort of thing a chump like that would do after sex. I slowly push the door open, until I can slip around it, and when I do, I see him.

There on the bed.

Covered.

Sleeping.

I hurt and I want him to hurt, but I'm in no frame of mind to take on a younger, fitter, leaner, man. I just want to curl up and cry. But I want him to pay, *first*. I take the knife and stand there over him. The knife up like some ceremonial dagger, over my head.

I plunge the blade down into his soft gut.

Pull it out and stab it down again.

And again.

This monster took my perfect wife in his own bed. I want him to pay, so I stab him again and again, countless times until his warm sticky guts are spilled over the bed like fucking porridge. Then I stop, his blood up my arms, over my shirt.

Shit.

I pull my clothing from me, and hurry downstairs. Dump it in the washer and put on a fast cycle. Then I return to the bedroom. It stinks now, like a copper mill. I pull his guts from his body. I drag his intestines out. I wrap the long coils of smooth mucosa around his wrists like a bondage play, and I tie him off to the bedposts with them. A hideous visage of gore, blood painting the bedroom, some monstrous artwork surrounding the monster himself. And I start to laugh.

I can't help it. Giggling, I leave the room, padding barefoot and naked, leaving a trail of blood behind me, I go to the shower and wash him from me.

Then I dry and go downstairs.

I have a cup of coffee while I wait for my clothes to dry. I'm not worried that his girlfriend will come home. I know she's at work because my wife was here, fucking her boyfriend without concern.

I wash my mug. Dress. Close the kitchen window I broke in through.

I let myself out of the front door to leave. A quick look around, and then back to the car.

Home.

Mrs. Jones

I watch Tracy leave, knowing she's going to find her boyfriend in bed, serenely laying in eternal sleep. Smiling to myself, I ready my things to go too. It's the best way for her. He could have just disappeared, and then she would be eternally fearful of his return, he could have beaten her to death over the state of his breakfast eggs. This was the best way. Find him dead in bed.

Yes.

I don't know why I try to convince myself it is for the best, but I do. Perhaps, because it is the first time I've done it for someone else, and not myself. That need that grows in me. I've tried looking it up online, and there doesn't appear to be a medical term. Black Widowosis. Something like that.

I pull my jacket on and head down to the car. In. Head towards home. I'll find out about Aaron from Tracy tomorrow, I'm sure. She won't come in, she'll phone. Blub down the phone at me and tell me that he's died some inexplicable death. Something no one can explain. The doctors are baffled.

Or some such.

Turning into my road, I check my makeup in the mirror. I want my husband. I want him badly. Even if he did have a strop on this morning. It doesn't matter. I've forgotten it now.

I pull up and look up at the house. Get from the car and go in. I toss my jacket on the stairs and go to the kitchen. No food. No wine. No Husband. I squint at the table. Now don't get me wrong, I don't *expect* him to be slaving over the cooker when I get home, but let's be fair ... it's *usual*. I turn on my heels. Look in the living room as I walk by to the bottom of the stairs. I know he had the arse, but this is most unlike him. I hope he's okay. I get to the bottom of the stairs and call up. "Honey, are you okay?" After a moment, he appears at the top of the stairs. He's out of his work clothes, in comfies. I smile, wave him forward. "I thought something had happened."

He shakes his head dismissively. "Nothing," he says. "Nothing important."

He comes down the stairs and passes me without a kiss. I watch him go. I must have really done something to piss him off. "I'm sorry," I say. It's instinctual. I don't owe any man anything, but I do love my husband, and I don't want him pissed.

"What for?" he asked.

"I don't know," I say, following him into the kitchen. He pulls open the fridge and stares inside. Grabs a pie and takes it to the counter, tossing it down.

"Pie?" he says.

"Fine," I reply. I don't really care. "Have I done something to upset you?"

He stares at me for a moment and then shakes his head. "Of course not," he says. A smile crosses his face.

I am not convinced.

Dinner was quieter than normal. He asked all the right questions, but it was the way he asked them. I felt like I was pulling teeth the whole time.

Then we retired to the living room and put the news on.

There was another murder. That serial killer again. I'm only half-watching it and half-watching him, but I notice that they're filming in the road where Tracy lives. I cast my eyes to the screen more than my husband and listen to the words. *It's Aaron.* Tracy is on TV. I think they've mistaken my little dalliance with him as the acts of the serial killer. How? How could they possibly do that?

Then the man on the TV says, middle of a sentence, "*... the young man found, brutally slain, his body ...*" he almost chokes over the words, "*... almost eviscerated.*"

I look at the screen in disbelief. "*Eviscerated,*" I say. I look at him, on the sofa next to me. I'm frowning. He's smiling.

"That's what the man said," he says.

I look back at the screen. I must have missed some pages somewhere ... what the fuck is happening? "That's Tracy's house," I say, pointing at the house behind the reporter.

"It is," he replies.

I look back to the screen, watching as it unfolds

outside this house, in this street, like it's a mistake or something.

My husband leans forward, into my line of sight. "Another drink?" he says.

I glance and nod, silently holding out my glass for him to take, which he does, and as he's standing, he says, "Lucky really, that the poor boy was still in bed, you know, for the killer … stringing him up with his own guts like that." Then he goes to the cabinet and pours another drink. Brings it back and hands it to me like he hadn't said anything. I do, however, note that we are sitting at opposite ends of the sofa. Not that I have time to worry about that. I return my look to the screen and keep watching.

They never said any of that which he just regurgitated. I'm sure of it. They said eviscerated. I watch him carefully out of the corner of my eye, and then when the news finishes he puts a film on like it's nothing.

We watch it, he loosens up a little, but still doesn't give anything away. When he catches me staring at him, trying to make up my mind, he says, "What?" like it's nothing.

Then we go to bed. We don't fuck. And now I'm laying here, wondering. Did my husband eviscerate Aaron? After I killed him? Fuck. It's ludicrous, of course. But laying in the dark I can put the pieces together. His ankle. The news said the man jumped from a window. Aaron … was he trying to defile the corpse to prove a point, or did he do it to cover up what I'd done? Which would be … good, *right*? I squint into the darkness, listening to him snore gently.

I don't know anymore.

Suddenly the darkness of the bedroom is surrounding me. I don't feel safe in my bed. In my skin. My husband, above all else, appears to be a serial killer. And he might well know I'm a black widow.

MR. JONES

I awake before the alarm goes off and just lie there for a while. I can hear my wife breathing. I don't know if she's asleep or not. It's very hard to tell. I look, she's facing away from me, but I don't touch her. I slip from the sheets and head downstairs.

I wonder what she's been thinking. Did she think that I cut him up because I'm a jealous and angry husband? Or did she think I did it because I'm a madman? Of course, she might have not put two and two together and still think it is some bizarre coincidence that a serial killer breaking modus operandi killed her long-time lover in a fit of rage.

I smile to myself, making coffee. I make hers too, without even thinking about it. Flipping through my phone I check the news, just in case there's been a breakthrough in the story. There's not. The police have issued a bland statement saying nothing.

They are most likely ridiculously confused.

Even *I* didn't expect me to kill a guy. That will be a turn up for the boffins. *Yes*, they were saying, I imagine, *a sadist killer, sexual of course. Primal in his sexuality, an alpha. That's why he's killing women. Asserting dominance. Power.*

Now?

They'll be staring over their glasses at the reports, scratching their chins. I don't know for sure, but maybe killing that man-whore was the best thing I could have done. Throw the law off completely. But now I have to wait before I do it again. That woman, the day before yesterday and him ... that's enough for now. I can't do it again. Not for a while. Maybe months. Years. Let them think it stopped as quickly as it started.

I stir my coffee and stand, looking out the window into the back. There are leaves rustling across the grass, which has overgrown. I've been too busy. Things have gotten away from me.

That first time was a blast. I was away on business and me and the boys had gotten tanked up in a bar in the evening. It was supposed to be a conference, but that quickly turned to a three day piss up. It was the last night and I was excited to come home. We all went to a restaurant, and Dave suggested we go to a bar afterwards, to have a drink and celebrate our new found friendship. I haven't spoken to Dave since. He might be dead for all I know. Anyway, Dave chooses the bar. I don't know until this day if he knew there was going to be callgirls there.

An odd experience ... not one I've had before or since. I was sitting at the bar, waiting on the next round when a girl came up to me. She flirted, and I flirted back thinking nothing of it, until she made her move.

I had never even considered being unfaithful.

But she threw herself at me and therefore couldn't be considered my fault, now, could it? Anyway, we ended up back at my hotel. It was a decent hotel because the company paid for it. In the room she said I could do anything I wanted. I'd always wanted to tie a girl up, and had never had the gumption to ask, so between the alcohol and the fact that I was never likely to see this girl again. I did.

She let me. I loved it. I can't lie.

I've never thought myself dominant, but there you go. These days I'll do whatever my wife wants—which can be pretty weird on her birthday—so I guess I'm submissive. Not that it makes a difference. Anyway. I was about to stick my dick in her and she tells me I can have her arse if I want. Now that *was* new. I'd never done that. Then she adds it'll be extra. *Extra?* I say. *Whatever do you mean?*

The penny drops before she says it, and I realise I've been bamboozled into sleeping with a prostitute. So, I guess I'm taking the hit. And I start to fuck her anyway. She grunts and groans like I'm a fucking stallion, and as I'm getting ready to finish, I put hand down on her chest but she says it's too high and I'm choking her.

I don't know what happened then. Something fired inside of me, and I kept fucking her and started to really choke her. I can still see the look in her eyes now. When I close my eyes and think about it. That look as she stares up at the ceiling. The life gone from her as I plough into her *surprisingly* tight fanny.

I sip my coffee, hearing my wife enter the kitchen behind me.

Hiding the body was the fun part. She was a whore. No one was going to report her missing were they?

I turn. Tip my cup in the direction of hers. "Sleep well?" I ask.

She nods and takes the drink. Bustling about. "I've got to go into work early," she says.

Yes, I expect you do. Make up for that time out yesterday. I nod at her. "Have a good day."

She puts the coffee down, half finished and leaves without attempting to kiss me goodbye. I know she knows I know, then. *That she's been fucking this guy for what could be months*. I shake my head and turn back to the window. Finish my coffee in peace, thinking about that whore. The look on her face. Dead. It was weird, though. I couldn't come. My body didn't allow it, even though it felt so good. I fucked the corpse for a good fifteen minutes after, without finishing.

And when I stopped, I could feel this wash of power over me. That was when I knew that it wasn't about sex. It was about being in control. About taking what I wanted without question.

———

As I stare into Excel, I can't help by think about the bullhorn outside. The police. Something is preying in the back of my mind. I know I've thrown the police a curve ball. It's something else. My subconscious trying to tell me something.

Something about my wife.

I push the chair back. It's time for a break, anyway.

Downstairs, I pass Gerald. He seems super invested in cat business, so I don't stop him. Let him *take out the garbage* or whatever is going through his little head. He's so cute. I hit the kitchen and grab a roll from the fridge. Rip it open and smear peanut butter in, a dob of mayo, and some cheese. Close the bap and go to the living room. I sit, and eat the tasty sandwich. I think about putting the TV on, but I don't. I just leave it, and sit in silence, wondering what I should be thinking about.

It's her, isn't it?

It's that she knows I'm the killer and she's a malignant bitch, fat with treachery.

It's that, isn't it?

She knows who I am and she's probably going to call the police.

M R S .   J O N E S

On the way into the office, my mind races. It might be because I only had two hours sleep and that was shit, too. I turn at the lights, not paying that much attention, and then right, towards the office. I'm going to assume he's killed all those people. It's the only reasonable assumption, isn't it? So I have two choices. I can tell the police, and let them deal with it. That, or I can tell him I know and talk it out. I can let bygones be bygones.

What the fuck are bygones?

I shake my head. I'm not thinking straight. Who the fuck cares. I can look it up later. I turn into the underground car park. I can't really tell the police, can I? I fucking adore my husband. But if I don't I'll have to tell him, otherwise he'll think I was fucking Aaron for fun. A shudder runs down my spine at the thought.

So I'll tell him *I can't help it*. I have to fuck them and kill them. If I don't I'll go mad. There's no rhyme nor reason to it. He'll have to understand, because he's the same, right? But what if he doesn't? What if he just thinks I'm a monster and calls the police?

He can't do that.

I pull into my space. I don't know. My mind is racing … between lack of sleep and this hell bent need I suddenly find myself with to come clean.

I go up the stairs, and to the office. A few of them are in before me today. I'm clearly not as early as I thought. So I sit at my desk and think.

I don't even realise Tracy has come in.

She smiles and sits. I smile back, unaware of my actions. I think my brain might be rebelling on my body and I might be about to have a breakdown.

Then Lawrence puts a file down in front of me. "Needs a signature," he says.

I blink at it. What?

"Are you okay?"

"Yes, sorry, long night." I sign the papers, whatever they are and then watch Tracy for a moment. Some of the staff must have seen the news because they all coo quietly over her. I can see though, below the surface, she's less tense. She's come into work because she's happy he's dead. Which is good. That was the whole point of it, anyway.

I settle into my chair and try to actually do something. I read words from the screen, but I don't take them in. What am I going to do? What if he's planning on killing me? What if he can't help himself?

———

The day passes without any huge problems and I even stumble through my lunch break at my desk still half-working. Still confused.

And when everyone else has left I just sit there. I should go home. Being late for no reason will only make things worse. If he thinks I've been having an affair, which is a strong possibility I suppose, he at least knows it's over. I get up and walk to the lift. Taking that down to the car park. I guess all I can do is judge when I get home.

I'm going to have to explain the reason to him. One way or the other. It goes back to before we met. I was in a club. Late teens. You know how it was back then. I was dancing with the girls and this guy comes up to me. He's charming in a *trying to pick up girls* sort of way, and we get on, and after a quick fumble in the corner he suggests that we go for a walk. You know. Get away from all these people. Which I'm on board with. Along the seafront maybe. A quick smooch in the bus stop.

But he had other ideas. We strolled, his arm around me, chatting about nothing, when I was suddenly fronted with his door. He'd guided me to his place. Asks me in for a drink. Like I said, I was young. I didn't realise that going home with a stranger, not telling my friends where I was … these were all bad things. I didn't even have a mobile phone.

And before I knew it he was trying to take my clothes from me. We weren't in the bedroom or anything, and I was wanting a drink. The walk had sobered me up. He said he didn't have anything to drink, but he had something better, and whipped out his cock.

I don't know. In retrospect it would have been a better idea for me to scream rape at the top of my voice. I didn't want to have sex with him, but I didn't feel like I had any option. He would say I was up for it. I *was* in his flat at midnight. Tipsy, and silly. So I let him fuck me. He wasn't good, and didn't care about me. Much like Aaron, I guess. If boys are going to be like that, why don't they just stay at home and jerk off? It must be easier, cheaper, and less dangerous. What with infections and all, and back then there were some nasty ones.

He didn't use protection.

When he'd finished he heaved and huffed, slumped in the chair opposite the sofa and lit a cigarette. Like he was some Fabio, or something. I didn't speak. I just went and found the bathroom and showered him off me. Washed his seed from my legs. I didn't understand back then that he'd assaulted me. I thought, because I was too scared to stop him, he was right to do it.

But I didn't want him to get away with it scot-free. So I when I was clean I stopped by the kitchen and looked for something to threaten him with. Scare him I suppose. I took this metal mallet looking thing. It was for tenderising meat.

I took it and I waved it at him. In the living room, while he watched me—I told him he needed to respect women. He was grinning. I was naked. I didn't think about it, but I suppose I wasn't very threatening.

So I step forward and tenderised his forehead. The skin split open with the first strike, the *crack* of the bone filling the room with sound. He grunted and slumped and started to fit. So I hit him again, to stop him. I don't know what I was thinking, but I hit him and hit him and hit him until he stopped having a fit. His head looking like a dog chew toy made out of meat.

Blood and flesh torn by the mallet, hanging from his head, half-degloved. Eyeballs popped and drooling this viscous see-through liquid. Breathing hard, I stopped. I felt like a million dollars. It was incredible. A feeling of power, and wealth, and I ... I can barely explain.

The doors to the lift open and I step out, going to the car.

I felt like I'd never felt before. I didn't do it again, not like that. I wasn't caught, obviously, but I was scared that a brutal attack like that would still be in someone's cold case files to this day. Waiting for them to knock on the door. Take me from my husband in handcuffs for the murder of some rapist. But I just had to chase that feeling. Months would go by and I didn't need it ... then one morning I would wake up, and the need, the desire was there.

When I married I assumed it would go. I certainly never had the desire to do it to *him*. But again, home from the honeymoon for a few weeks and I woke up one morning. There it was. I had to kill.

I start the engine and head towards home.

I'm going to play tonight by ear, and keep my fingers crossed. I don't know what to expect.

———

When I pull the car up, I look at the house. Wondering what to expect. I let myself in the front door and drop my jacket down.

I watch him through the door into the kitchen.

I can smell dinner.

I stroll down the hallway to the kitchen, and I open the door. He's there, in a shirt, and trousers. He's preparing dinner. There's a glass of wine on the table and so I sit. I take a sip, watch his arse as he bends to the oven and removes the chicken. Pokes it and puts it back.

"Won't be long," he says. He lifts his own glass of wine to his lips watching me as he sips from it.

We share a smile, looking into each other's eyes in silence for a moment. I can't tell what he's thinking, I never have been able to, but I know he's thinking something. Dinner is a pleasant surprise, though. Maybe he's not angry. Maybe he *was* covering for me. I'll wait, and see how it plays out.

We sit and talk about nothing for a while, waiting for the chicken to finish. He asks how my day was and I ask about his and neither of us say anything that matters. The same happens over dinner. I have a growing doubt. He might not be tackling the subject because it's to be swept under the table. He covered my kill—he understands me—we're one in the same. But he could also be seething with anger that I fucked another man. That I betrayed him. I don't know which it is.

And I'm afraid.

The more we don't talk about it the more afraid I am.

After dinner we go to the living room and he sits in the corner of the sofa intimating that we should sit together. I lay into his cleft like I have done a thousand times and everything is fine. We watch the news. It barely mentions my husband, the killer, and then we watch a film. Laugh over the silly action.

Back to the way we were. Only a few short days ago.

Then we go upstairs. I take my handbag and put it beside the bed, and when I go to the bathroom, as he comes out, he kisses me. Deeply, our tongues touching, gentle at first, and then fiercely, like we've been apart for months. The bathroom forgotten, I take his hand and pull him, back to the bedroom. A deep, burning, insatiable lust within me. I stop him at the bed, and I pull his shirt open, slowly, revealing his torso beneath. As I undo button after button, I bite and lick his skin, listening to him hiss as I do, the pleasure oozing from him. I pull the shirt from his shoulders. Drop it to the floor behind us. Then I drop to my knees. I look up at him and open his belt, yanking it free, then his trousers, his erection forcing its way out, tight beneath his underwear. Then I pull those down too. Taking his girth in my lips.

He groans in delight, puts his fist into my hair, taking a handful and pulling me up to my feet. He turns us like we're dancing and with my back to the bed, he pushes me, over onto my back. Over me, he pulls my shirt off, tearing it, animal urges taking him over. He's not been like this in forever. He rips my bra from me, and pulls my skirt up over my hips. Panties down. He parts my lips with his fingers and tongues at my clit, heat rising in me. I can't help by feel my orgasm tighten.

But he stops.

Pulls my panties down the rest of the way, and climbs over me. He positions himself to fuck me and I guide his cock, rigid, inside me. He slides deep and we both let out a gasp as he pulls back, then pushes forward. Slowly at first. That orgasm he found, rising with each stoke. Harder. And harder.

"Fuck me," I say. "Henry, fuck me."

He does, he pushes and pulls and brings an orgasm from me, as I tighten my legs around his arse, he strokes faster, and faster. I can feel him pulsing inside of me, getting closer himself. He pushes himself up, his hand tight on my breasts, then off, he puts them around my throat, squeezing as he fucks. I stare up at him. Fear, gripping me. Another orgasm brought on by his girth, my trepidation as he chokes me, fucking me, harder and harder. I look into his eyes and see the anger in there. His fingers tight enough to stop the air now. A third orgasm bursts though me as a ring of black circles my vision. I'm losing my thoughts. Only pleasure and pain now. I can't think as he comes inside of me, a darkness swimming over my sight ... my thoughts.

Then a flood of air as he releases me and drops to his elbows. On me. I gasp air in. He's touching me, fondling and licking and kissing, but I can barely feel any of it, so close to blacking out. The darkness subsides and lets me breathe life back into *me*. He speaks, but it sounds like I'm underwater.

Then he rolls to his side and gets from the bed. Leaving the room, naked. To the bathroom, I imagine. My head spins still. I don't know how to think. I wait, for the calm, the lull. And when I can, I think that he knows, and he's just shown me who is in charge.

A silent warning.

I know, now, that he has me on a string. Dangling. Where I will be without doubt for the rest of my life. And that, I'm sure, is unacceptable. I roll to the side and swing my legs from the bed. I'm woozy. I feel drunk. Waiting for my senses to return, proper. I grab my handbag from beside the bed and fumble inside. Pull the bottle of spiked whiskey from the folds.

I pour him a healthy double into the glass by the bed. Then I return the bottle to the bag, and drop it to the floor. Pushing it under the bed with my foot. The room, slowly swaying less.

Pushing myself up against the pillow, I lay there, naked, sprawled, waiting for his return. I pray that I am not too late, for my own sake.

He comes back and smiles at me. Like nothing has just happened. Like the power in the relationship hasn't swung and I'm supposed to be a helpless damsel. Well. *I'm not*. He slides onto the bed and takes my breast in his hand, his face stooping down low to cup my nipple with his mouth, suckling on me.

I feel nothing. My life has turned upside down,

and whatever he was hoping to achieve by choking me, all he's done is drive me further away than I had been before. *Not that I think he noticed.*

MR. JONES

"Here," Bell says, handing me a tumbler of whiskey. "I got you this."

I pull from her teet, and take the glass. I didn't realise I had been pissing for that long. She swings from under me and gets to her feet. "I'm going to quickly shower." Then she goes. Shame. I was up for round two. I watch her go. Her arse, wiggling in that way that it does.

Round two, *before I finish this*.

She's acting out. She's fucking some other man. *Was* fucking, I correct myself. And she knows I'm a killer. Probably thinks I was going to kill her too, but honestly, I wasn't. *But I am now*.

I thought I would show her how I could at any point. Choke her while she came. But that changed everything. That look in her eyes ... it was true fear. She *really* thought I was going to kill her there in the bed, while I was fucking her. Maybe I should have? Just done it without thought and phoned the police myself. *Death by Misadventure*. Choked out in sex play. I could get a good attorney. I could get away with it, I'm sure. But I didn't. A misstep on my part.

I'll correct it, now. I hold the glass of harsh brown liquid to my lips. Smelling the savoury flavours. Then I place it down on the side table. I get from the bed. I think everything will be easier if I just do away with her now. I won't wait. If I do, I might have *feelings* and regret it.

Besides. I felt something then in bed that I haven't felt before.

Before I ... I don't know ... that feeling of power as I took their lives, their beating hearts slowing to a stop. Even the desecration of the bodies ... it felt so raw, so visceral. I can feel the power flowing through me when I do it.

But that? That feeling *while* I'm fucking them. That is something else.

And I can't be cheating on Bell like that. Between her treachery, and that I want *that* feeling? I don't see myself having a choice.

I can hear the shower running.

Going along the hall, I watch her. She's showering under hot water. Far hotter than I could. The bathroom filling with steam. I suppose I could have her *slip in the shower*. That would alleviate questions, I suppose. But what if I set it up wrong? I could go down for twenty years for that and never feel that strength again. The power of fucking someone as I snuff out their light. Not until I got out and I was an old man. I could do her, and hide the body. An old fashioned kill? I suppose that would work. I could do her my way, and feign coming home and finding her like that.

Yes.

That would put me the middle of the investigation as a victim. That could really work.

She turns the shower off and steps out, glistening, to the mat on the floor. She takes a towel and starts to dab at herself.

I want to feel it. I want that feeling when the heart stops beating as I come. And I'm not going to wait for it. I don't know if I can wait days or weeks before I'm out from under the spotlight of the police to be safe enough to do it to someone else.

I'm standing, leaning against the doorframe when she swipes the mirror with a towel, brushing the steam from it and sees me. Gives a little jump and laughs. She turns, and drops the towel.

"How was your drink?" she asks.

I grunt a response. I don't want to seem ungrateful. I suppose I could do both. I could do it to her now, and then call the police. Say she was like it when I got home.

Walking across the bathroom to her at the sink. When I get close enough she grabs at my cock, desperate for it, it seems. Maybe she's more down with me being like I am than she'd want to admit. But I can't put her through having to watch me fuck other women, over and over. My mind is made up.

My cock is already hard.

"Was it nice?" she asks.

She's still talking about that drink? Fucking hell. "Great," I say. Pacify her. I put my hands on her shoulders and turn her to the sink. Facing the mirror. I look in her eyes as I stuff my cock inside her. She grins, and I know she loves it. Forcing myself back and forth. She puts her hands down on the counter, one each side of the sink. My thrusts faster, the feeling growing on me. My hands slide up to her neck. Fingers around the front, thumbs at the back. I thrust harder.

Start to squeeze.

She watches me like she's waiting for something at first. Like she's waiting for me to stop. But I don't. I pump harder into her, choking her harder. And harder. Her eyes grow wild when she realises what I'm doing and she starts to struggle, but it's no good. She's impaled and my hands are tight around her neck. My body weight on her. She puts her hands against the mirror trying to push back against me, but it only serves to push me deeper inside her.

Her air gasping in short, tight breaths.

Short and tight, just how I like it. I squeeze harder and they stop. Her airways blocked. I fuck her hard. Trying to bring a second orgasm out. I'm not as young as I used to be but when she looks me in the eyes in the mirror, and the light just dims, I can feel it there. And as the light extinguishes, I come.

Her fingers slide down the mirror. As I pump once, twice, three times, finishing the best orgasm of my life.

I slump over her, the two of us leaning naked on the sink. Then I slide from her, my cold cum drooling down the inside of her flesh. I step back and draw air in through my nose, eyes shut, savouring this new feeling.

Yes. There will be many, many more of these.

After a moment, I open my eyes and study the

corpse. This one should be special. I turn her, and lower her to the bathroom floor. Put her legs together and her arms out, like she's diving from a board into the warm pool. I get my cutthroat razor from the cupboard, and I slit her open. Neck to vagina. The blood, still warm inside her is easy to work with, and I use my fingers to paint a heart on the floor below her.

When I stand, I can truly admire the art.

Then I shower, and leave the bathroom, careful not to disturb the body, or the painting.

Back to the bedroom. I need to make it look like I just got home. So I start to dress, back in my regular clothes. Shit. What was my reason for not being here? I collect my thoughts. Think like a husband. Wife's coming home … something nice?

No. *Think* damn it. We've already eaten. I look at the whiskey she'd poured. That's it. A romantic evening.

I go downstairs and get the whiskey bottle from the cabinet. Pour it down the sink.

Then I head out. Down to the off licence where I purchase a new bottle. Lay it on thick with the clerk about how great my evening is going and how much I love my wife.

Then I return home.

Take the bottle upstairs. I put it on the bed, and go to the bathroom. Just one last look. She's getting pale now. I can't waste time. But seeing her like that, knowing what I'd done, it turns me on. After all said and done, all those times the police thought I was escalating ... turns out I *was*.

I go back to the bedroom and pull my phone. I make some *wah* noises, preparing myself, before I dial the nines.

"What service do you require?"

"The police," I scream. "It's my wife. She's been ... been ..." My acting isn't great, but when they arrive here in a while, the body will help sell it. I'm put through to the police, and I lay it on as thick as I can. "She's dead," I say. "There's blood everywhere," I plead. "It was *him*," I scream. It's pretty Shakespearian.

And then I give them my address and I hang up. Sit on the bed. I look at the whiskey in the bottle. I nod, appreciating my own work. Rub my eyes hard, trying to make them red.

I run lines like I'm due on stage. "I just went out. We were having a romantic evening and we ran out of whiskey. I just went down the road. I couldn't have been gone more than a few minutes." It was twenty three. I did keep count. That should sell it to them. I don't think I've missed anything.

I pick up the glass of whiskey from the bedside table and I take a sip. I go to the window and I look out, waiting for the police. Another sip. The whiskey is warming and helps.

I imagine the police outside. All the cars there. But this time there's no bullhorn. Just an ambulance to take the body.

Prologue

"Looks like someone broke in while he was at the offy, Guv." I keep my attention on Detective Davies. I'm up for transfer into plain clothes and I want to make a good impression. He's crouched next to the body.

"Anything else?" he says standing.

I follow as he goes through to the bathroom. "Woman looks like she was cut up real bad. I don't want to make assumptions but—"

"Then don't," he interrupts.

"It's different," I say, as we look down on the woman. She's naked and spliced open. A razor discarded to the side. "Looks like he had a heart attack after calling it in."

Davies crouches down by the second body. "He's escalating again," he says.

I'd say so. Look at the mess.

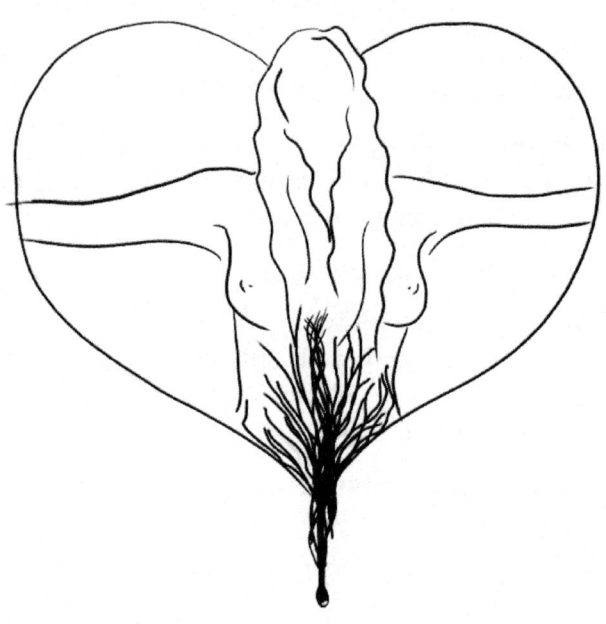

About the Author

Ash is a British horror author. He resides in the south, in the Garden of England. He writes horror that is sometimes fantastical, sometimes grounded, but always deeply graphic, and black with humour.

www.ashericmore.com

Printed in Great Britain
by Amazon